Slippers ~at~ Home

by **Andrew Clements**
illustrated by **Janie Bynum**

PUFFIN BOOKS

For Matthew and Tricia Clements,
whose love for their dogs has brought joy and inspiration to so many
A.C.

To Mo, who loves her puppies!
XO, J.B.

PUFFIN BOOKS
Published by the Penguin Group
Penguin Young Readers Group, 345 Hudson Street, New York, New York 10014, U.S.A.
Penguin Group (Canada), 90 Eglinton Avenue East, Suite 700,
Toronto, Ontario, Canada M4P 2Y3 (a division of Pearson Penguin Canada Inc.)
Penguin Books Ltd, 80 Strand, London WC2R 0RL, England
Penguin Ireland, 25 St Stephen's Green, Dublin 2, Ireland (a division of Penguin Books Ltd)
Penguin Group (Australia), 250 Camberwell Road, Camberwell, Victoria 3124, Australia (a division of Pearson Australia Group Pty Ltd)
Penguin Books India Pvt Ltd, 11 Community Centre, Panchsheel Park, New Delhi - 110 017, India
Penguin Group (NZ), Cnr Airborne and Rosedale Roads, Albany, Auckland 1310, New Zealand (a division of Pearson New Zealand Ltd)
Penguin Books (South Africa) (Pty) Ltd, 24 Sturdee Avenue, Rosebank, Johannesburg 2196, South Africa

Registered Offices: Penguin Books Ltd, 80 Strand, London WC2R 0RL, England

First published in the United States of America by Dutton Children's Books, a division of Penguin Young Readers Group, 2004
Published by Puffin Books, a division of Penguin Young Readers Group, 2007

1 2 3 4 5 6 7 8 9 10

Text copyright © Andrew Clements, 2004
Illustrations copyright © Janie Bynum, 2004
All rights reserved

THE LIBRARY OF CONGRESS HAS CATALOGED THE DUTTON CHILDREN'S BOOKS EDITION AS FOLLOWS:
Clements, Andrew, date.
Slippers at home / by Andrew Clements; illustrated by Janie Bynum.—1st ed. p. cm.
Summary: Slippers the puppy loves each of the four people who share his home.
ISBN: 0-525-47138-3 (hc)
[1. Dogs—Fiction. 2. Animals—Infancy—Fiction. 3. Human-animal relationships—Fiction. 4. Dwellings—Fiction.]
I. Bynum, Janie, ill. II. Title.
PZ10.3.C5937Sli 2004 [E]—dc22 2003027885

Puffin Books ISBN 978-0-14-240781-3

Manufactured in China
Designed by Beth Herzog

Slippers has a little house of his own.

His little house sits inside a bigger house.

Slippers likes his little house, and he likes
his big house, too.

In his big house Slippers has four people.

There is an Edward.

There is a Laura.

There is a Mommy.

And there is a Daddy.

Slippers is glad he has four people of his very own, and he loves every one of them.

Edward is the boy who lives in the big house with Slippers. Edward is not much bigger than Slippers. Edward walks around on four paws, just like Slippers does.

Slippers can always tell when Edward is coming.
Edward is LOUD. He squeals. He gurgles.
He babbles. But most of all, Edward laughs
and laughs and laughs.

Edward likes to do the things that Slippers likes to do.

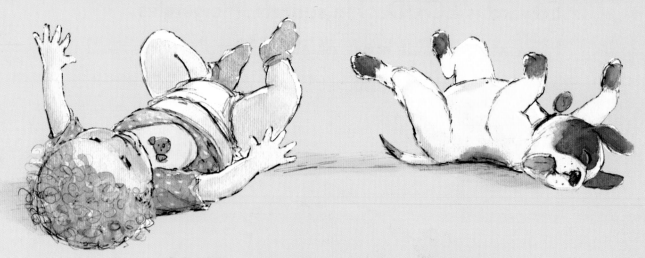

He likes to roll around on the floor.

He likes to push a ball with his nose.

He likes to look out the window.

And Edward loves to chew on things.

Sometimes Edward crawls right in to visit
Slippers in his little house.

They play games like pull-the-sock and
share-the-cookie.

And sometimes Edward curls up on the pillow with Slippers, and they take a little nap together.

Slippers loves Edward, and Edward loves him right back.

Laura is the girl who lives in the house with Slippers. Laura is bigger than Edward, and she is MUCH bigger than Slippers.

She walks around on two paws. It makes her very tall.

Laura has her own place in the big house.
It is a long way from the little house where
Slippers lives.

To find the Laura place, Slippers sniffs
and sniffs and sniffs the air. And when
he sniffs Laura, he follows his nose.

He sniffs his way out the
door of his little house.
He sniffs his way down
the long, long hall.

He sniffs his way across
the slippy-slidey kitchen.

He sniffs his way across
the soft rug.

Then he sniffs his way up and up and up the stairs. And at the top of the stairs, Slippers finds the Laura place.

Slippers likes to play in the Laura place.

He plays hide-the-pencil.
He plays chew-the-shoe.

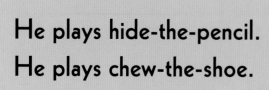

He plays bite-the-paper.

He plays sleep-
in-the-sweater.

Sometimes Laura does not like the way
that Slippers plays.

But when Slippers looks up at her, Laura always smiles. Then Laura lifts Slippers way up high and hugs him.

And Laura always gives Slippers a free ride all the way back to his own little house.

Mommy is the lady who lives in the big house with Slippers. Mommy is so big that she can carry Edward and Slippers at the same time.

Slippers loves to follow Mommy around the slippy-slidey kitchen. When Mommy makes the supper sizzle, Slippers loves to sniff and sniff and sniff.

Two times a day, Mommy makes the round sounds. First there is the sound of the big round bowl. Then there is the sound of the nice round can.

Into the can goes the long round spoon.
Out comes the food into the big round bowl.

Then the food from the big round bowl goes into the little round tummy.

And that little round tummy belongs to . . .

SLIPPERS!

Once a week Mommy lifts Slippers onto a table.
Starting up front at his sniffy black nose, Mommy
gives Slippers a brush, brush, brushing—all the
way back to his waggy white tail.

Then Mommy says to Edward and Laura, "Isn't Slippers the most handsome puppy in the whole wide world?"

And Edward and Laura always say, "YES!"

Daddy is the man who lives in the big house
with Slippers.

Daddy is so big that Slippers can
almost hide in one of his boots.

When Daddy reads a book to Edward and Laura, he always says, "Hey, you two, make some room for Slippers!" Then Slippers gets to sit on Daddy's lap, too.

Every night Daddy takes Slippers out. The world outside the house is so big. Slippers can't tell where it begins or where it ends. Slippers walks close to Daddy. Sometimes they walk so far that Slippers has to sit down and rest.

But no matter how far they go, Daddy always finds the way back home.

He takes Slippers inside and wipes off his feet one by one.

Then he puts Slippers into his little house, and he scratches him behind the ears, and he says, "Good night, Slippers. I'll see you tomorrow."

Every night it gets very quiet in the big house. Slippers sits in his little house and listens, and everything sounds just right.

Then Slippers goes to the door of his little house, and he sniffs four times.

He sniffs once, and he knows that Daddy is in the big house.

He sniffs again, and he knows that Mommy is in the big house.

He sniffs a third time, and he knows that Laura is in the big house.

Then he sniffs one last time, and he knows that Edward is in the big house.

And as Slippers lies down to sleep in his
little house, he knows why he is so happy.

Slippers has four people of his very own,
and he loves every one of them.